SANTA ANA PUBLIC LIBRARY

3 1994 01551 9140

D0499133

Science, Maker, and Real Technology Students

S.M.A.R.T.S.

S.M.A.R.T.S. is published by Stone Arch Books
A Capstone Imprint
1710 Roe Crest Drive
North Mankato, MN 56003
www.capstonepub.com

Text and illustrations © 2016 Stone Arch Books

All rights reserved. No part of this publication may be reproduced in whole
or in part, or stored in a retrieval system, or transmitted in any form or by
any means, electronic, mechanical, photocopying, recording, or otherwise,
without written permission of the publisher.

Library of Congress Cataloging-in-Publication Data is available on the Library
of Congress website.

ISBN: 978-1-4965-0464-7 (hardcover) -- 978-1-4965-0472-2 (paperback) --
978-1-4965-2341-9 (eBook PDF)

Summary: Kids are getting sick during lunch . . . and it's not because of
questionable cafeteria food. It's poison! When there's a school mystery that
needs solving, the S.M.A.R.T.S. are ready to put their sharp minds to the
test! It will take their best critical-thinking skills and scientific reasoning to
get to the bottom of this lunch period puzzle.

Designer: Hilary Wacholz

Printed in China by Nordica
0415/CA21500550
032015   008838NORDF15

S.M.A.R.T.S.

AND THE POISON PLATES

By Melinda Metz

Illustrated by Heath McKenzie

STONE ARCH BOOKS
a capstone imprint

1

Zoe Branson held up her cell phone as she recorded video. "I'm getting an establishing shot," she said. "That's what it's called in a movie when you focus on the setting. I read about it online last night."

She and her two best friends, Jaden Thompson and Caleb Quinn, were standing in the cafeteria line at second lunch on Tuesday. Sometimes waiting for the second lunch period was a real pain. But that's just how it was. First lunch was for seventh and eighth graders; second lunch was for fifth and sixth graders.

"Make sure to get in all the tables and the food line, everything in the whole room, all the people too," Caleb said.

Zoe nodded and scanned the room with her phone, feeling like a big-time Hollywood director.

"But we're going to be using still photographs to make our movie," Jaden reminded her. "We're not filming it."

The movie was their latest assignment for S.M.A.R.T.S. The club, which stood for Science, Maker, and Real Technology Students, had started at Hubble

Middle School at the beginning of the year. At their most recent meeting, their fifth-grade science teacher and club advisor, Mrs. Ramanujan — Mrs. Ram for short — had announced they'd be split into groups to make stop-motion animation movies.

With stop-motion, they could make movies where it looked like action figures or other objects were moving around by themselves. All they had to do was take a picture of whatever object they decided to use, move it a tiny bit, take another picture, move it a tiny bit, and keep on repeating that about a hundred times. Then they would use special computer software that would take all the pictures and combine them into a movie.

"This is still good practice," Zoe replied, continuing to film. "We can use a lot of the same techniques for our movie." She lowered her phone. "I'll take some close-ups of the food when we get up there. I read last night that it's good to mix up the camera angles you use. When we take the pictures for our movie, we should move the camera around."

"If you're really going to show what the caf is like, you have to get some close-ups of the Ponies and the Inferior Five," Caleb told Zoe.

The Ponies — so named because they always wore their hair in identical ponytails — were the five most popular girls at school. At the other end of the popularity spectrum were the Inferior Five, a group of boys who loved comic books more than anything. They loved them so much that they'd formed a club and named it after the Inferior Five, a group of goofy superheroes from DC Comics who could solve crimes when they teamed up.

Zoe, Jaden, and Caleb loved comics almost as much as the Inferior Five did. It was one of the reasons the three of them had ended up as friends. Though they'd known each other since kindergarten, it wasn't until they'd joined S.M.A.R.T.S. at the beginning of the year that they'd realized how much they had in common — namely a love of comics, science fiction, video games, puzzles, and anything to do with science.

The Ponies and the Inferior Five had an ongoing competition during second lunch — more like a battle — over which group got to be first in line. No one else even bothered trying to get there first anymore.

The competition was pretty evenly matched. Three of the Inferiors had their last class before lunch two doors down from the caf. That gave them a leg up over everyone else.

But the Ponies had Emily Ward. Emily wasn't one of the Ponies, despite the fact that she always wore her wavy red hair in a ponytail. She was a Ponies wannabe, which meant she did all sorts of favors for the group in the hopes that they'd let her in — including getting in the lunch line first. And since Emily's last class before lunch was one door down from the cafeteria, she had a good head start.

If Emily made it to the cafeteria first, she'd save places for all the Ponies. And if an Inferior boy got there first, he'd save places for all the others in his group. Today the Ponies had won.

"I'm not sure the Ponies would let me take close-ups of them," Zoe admitted. The Ponies might be the most popular girls, but they weren't the nicest. They'd said lots of mean things to lots of kids at school.

"Maybe I could do it for you," Jaden offered. "They're okay to me."

Caleb snorted. "Okay? They love you. Everybody loves you." Jaden was one of the most popular, well-liked kids at school.

"That would be great," Zoe answered. "I'll give you my phone later when they're settled at their table."

The line moved forward, and Zoe got busy taking close-ups of the food. Today the cafeteria ladies were serving roasted chicken with rice and egg salad sandwiches on whole wheat buns. The side dishes were salad, baby carrots, and mashed potatoes, and for dessert there was a choice of chilled peaches or mixed fruit.

"Go for the peaches," someone said. Jaden looked up and saw Sonja, one of his fellow S.M.A.R.T.S., watching him from the kitchen side of the food counter. "The syrup is yummy to drink," she added.

"What are you doing back there?" Jaden asked. Students were never allowed in the kitchen.

"I wanted to ask if we could get popcorn for next week for the S.M.A.R.T.S. movie screenings," Sonja answered. "And we can!"

"Awesome possum," Zoe said, grabbing an egg salad sandwich.

"Could I have carrots?" Jaden asked the cafeteria lady. As she spooned some on his plate, he turned to his friends. "Hey, what sounds like a parrot?"

Zoe groaned. She knew Jaden well enough to recognize the start of one of his bad jokes. She had to limit him to three a day; her mind would melt if she had to hear more.

"A carrot!" Jaden exclaimed when neither Zoe nor Caleb answered.

Caleb shook his head, grabbed an apple juice, and headed to the cashier. That was the only thing he ever bought at the cafeteria. Tuna sandwiches, which he always brought from home, and apple juice were basically the only foods he liked.

After they'd all paid, Jaden, Zoe, and Caleb headed to a table and sat down. They'd already decided to use their lunch hour to start coming up with ideas for their movie.

"Hey, guys," Gabriel, one of the Inferior Five, called as he headed over to them. He handed each of them a flier with prices for a bunch of comics and collectibles. "I know you're all really into comics, so I wanted you to know I'm selling some stuff."

"Why are you getting rid of them?" Caleb asked.

Gabriel frowned and shrugged. "Just tired of them." With that, he started toward another table with the fliers.

"Weird," Jaden said. "Who gets tired of comics?"

"He's even dressing weird," Caleb added.

"What do you mean? He doesn't look weird to me," Zoe said. Gabriel had on cargo pants and a neatly pressed button-down shirt. "It's just basic department store stuff."

"Exactly!" Caleb exclaimed. "Gabriel used to go to the Goodwill and buy the goofiest T-shirts he could find. I went with him once. He found a shirt advertising a sewage and drain repair company. He loved it."

"Wearing a shirt with the word 'sewage' on it is what I'd call weird," Zoe said. She glanced across the room at Gabriel. "He changed his hair too. The boy has discovered product."

"Who cares what he's wearing? Let's get back to more important stuff — our movie," Jaden said. He took a bite of his chicken. "What should it be about?"

"That depends," Zoe said. "Do we want to use action figures and go with characters that already exist? Or do we want to make something of our own?"

"I say we make something," Caleb answered. "That's more original."

"Or maybe we could use something normal, like toothbrushes, and animate them. It'd be cool to see them move around," Jaden said.

"Like they have a secret life when people aren't watching," Zoe agreed, getting excited.

They kept tossing ideas around until Jaden saw Isabella, the most popular girl at school, stand up from the Ponies' table and hurry across the cafeteria.

"If you want close-ups of the Ponies, give me your phone," Jaden said. "It looks like Isabella's leaving."

Zoe handed Jaden her cell. "Why's she leaving now? Lunch isn't over for another ten minutes."

"You're trying to understand a Pony?" Caleb said. "That's impossible."

As Jaden stood up, Isabella suddenly broke into a run. Jaden followed more slowly. Because of his cerebral palsy, which made one of his legs stiff and weak, he had to wear leg braces to walk.

With a sharp cry, Isabella skidded to a stop in front of the trash can by the big double doors — and threw

up right into it. Ms. Padgett, one of the
cafeteria ladies, rushed toward her. But
she froze as one of the Inferior Five,
Leo, suddenly threw up onto his lunch
tray. Ms. Padgett didn't seem to know
which kid to go to first.

Before she could decide, Emily, the Ponies wannabe,
pressed her hands over her mouth and bolted across the
room. She made it through the doors without puking.
Ms. Padgett immediately hurried after her.

"I'm calling the nurse!" one of the other cafeteria
workers cried.

At the Inferiors' table nearby, Owen moaned. "My
stomach feels like it's going to explode!"

His older sister, Olivia, one of the Ponies, leaped up
from her group's table by the windows. She swayed back
and forth for a moment, then sank back down in her
seat, both hands pressed against her belly.

"What's going on?" Caleb exclaimed. "What's
happening to everybody?"

2

Ten minutes later, everything seemed to be under control. The school nurse had already gotten the sick kids down to her office. The cafeteria workers had started packing up the food.

"Kids, listen up!" Principal Romero called as she strode into the cafeteria. "Please don't eat anything else. It's possible something in the cafeteria food has made people sick."

"This is bad. Very bad," Caleb muttered. He ran his fingers through his dark hair. That's what he always did when he got agitated, and he got agitated a lot.

"We're going to temporarily close the cafeteria so we can figure out what happened here," Ms. Romero continued. "Please go on to your fourth-period classes. But if any of you start to feel nauseated or ill, please tell your teachers right away."

Sonja came over to their table. "Want to walk to English together?" she asked Zoe.

Zoe nodded. "See you guys at S.M.A.R.T.S. after school," she said to Caleb and Jaden.

"Unless we're too busy puking," Caleb muttered.

Zoe rolled her eyes. "You didn't even eat anything from the cafeteria," she reminded him. "You had your tuna."

"And apple juice." Caleb held up the open juice box.

Zoe wished she could think of something that would reassure him, but once Caleb got an idea in his head, it was almost impossible to talk him down. "Well, fingers, toes, and eyeballs crossed that we don't get sick," she finally said.

"I got a picture of Isabella heaving," Sonja said as they left the cafeteria and passed the trash can by the door.

"Really?" Zoe asked. It had all happened so fast. She was surprised Sonja had gotten a chance to grab her phone and snap a pic.

Sonja nodded. "I'm going to print it out and put it in my locker." She shot a look at Zoe. "I know that sounds horrible, but you don't know the things Isabella and the Ponies have said to me."

"I kind of do," Zoe admitted. "Isabella's been talking trash about my clothes and my hair and my everything else since she started at Hubble in the third grade. Last year when she formed the Ponies, it just got worse."

"I know!" Sonja exclaimed. "It's like five times the torture now. The other day I was in the bathroom with Emily and two of the other Ponies, and Emily splashed water on me in the bathroom and started saying I peed

my pants. They all started laughing like crazy. I know Emily did it to impress them. She wants to be one of them so badly, she'll do anything."

"Remember when Emily used to be nice?" Zoe asked.

Sonja scoffed. "Barely. But, yeah, we all used to hang out a couple years ago, back before Isabella got here."

Zoe nodded. "I wonder what made everyone get sick all at once," she said, changing the subject.

"I don't care. Whatever it is, I'm glad," Sonja declared. "Isabella deserved it. She deserves to have a million bad things happen to her — her and all her Ponies, including that wannabe, Emily."

Zoe stared at Sonja. It's not that she liked the Ponies. But wishing a million bad things would happen to them? Did Sonja really hate the Ponies *that* much?

3

That afternoon, after his last class had ended, Caleb strode into the makerspace. The community area at the back of the school's media center, which the S.M.A.R.T.S. used as their regular meeting place, housed all the equipment, tools, and supplies kids needed to work on robotics, science, and computer projects. Several of the other S.M.A.R.T.S. kids were already there.

"Ten!" Caleb burst out, holding up a crumpled piece of paper — a note from Principal Romero. His teacher had passed it out right before the last bell rang and asked all the students to pass it along to their parents. "Ten kids got sick in the cafeteria. That's what the note says." He'd only seen five get sick, and that was bad enough.

"The principal's note also said that there was no reason —" Benjamin, one of the S.M.A.R.T.S., began.

"— to believe the cafeteria food was responsible," his twin brother, Samuel, finished.

The twins, nicknamed "Thing One" and "Thing Two" after the Dr. Seuss characters, were always finishing each other's sentences. And it didn't stop there — they wore their hair exactly the same way and even dressed the same a lot of the time.

"But how can she say that?" Caleb demanded. "How can she really know that?"

The Things just shrugged in response.

"Principal Romero probably had the nurse or somebody check the food," Zoe suggested.

"Did you know every single one of the Ponies got sick? Emily too," Sonja added with a grin. She and two other S.M.A.R.T.S. kids were at a nearby table working on clay monsters for their movie.

Zoe shot a glance over at the other girl and frowned. Sonja seemed way too happy about the Ponies getting sick. Zoe shook her head and turned her attention back to the project she was working on with Caleb and Jaden. "So for our movie, what do you guys think about toothbrushes that become superheroes when no one is watching?"

Before Jaden or Caleb could answer, Mrs. Ram rushed in, her dark ponytail flying. "Sorry I'm late," she called. She glanced around the room. "I'm glad to see you all here. Too many people got sick today."

"Do you know why?" Caleb asked.

Mrs. Ram shook her head. "All I know is what Principal Romero wrote in the note for you to bring home to your parents. She's sure the cafeteria food wasn't responsible and that the school is safe. Now on to business! Or better yet, on to fun!"

Caleb wanted to know more, but before he could open his mouth, Mrs. Ram opened up a folder and took out a picture of a dog. She held it up, then took out a picture of a steak and held it up next to the first picture.

 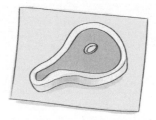

"What do you think when you look at these?" she asked the group.

"The dog wants to eat the steak," Sonja suggested.

Mrs. Ram replaced the picture of the steak with the picture of a tennis ball. "How about now?" she asked.

"The dog wants to play with the ball," Zoe called out.

Mrs. Ram smiled. "Exactly. This is an example of the power of film editing — putting two images next to each other," she told them. "The dog wasn't in the room with the steak or the ball when the picture was taken. The three pictures could have been taken years apart. But when you look at the pictures together, your mind makes a connection between them. The dog wants a steak. The dog wants a ball."

The teacher began pacing around the makerspace the way she always did when she got excited about a topic. "As you work on your movies, think about that concept," Mrs. Ram continued. "If you show a toy car heading toward a pile of blocks, then cut to the blocks in a heap, the person watching the movie will make the connection. They'll know the car ran into the blocks, even if you don't show the actual crash. The sequence of pictures tells the story."

"Awesome," Caleb said. He'd finally stopped thinking about people getting sick.

"So awesome," Mrs. Ram agreed. "We'll go over more film techniques you can use every time we meet. Then next Friday is movie day! We'll watch everyone's movie — with popcorn." That got cheers and applause from all the S.M.A.R.T.S.

Mrs. Ram looked around the room. "Any group need me right away?" Benjamin and Samuel both shot their hands up. "Okay, I'll come around to the rest of you once I finish with Benjamin and Samuel."

"If we do something with toothbrushes, maybe we could start with real ones, then switch to ones made out of clay when they come alive," Jaden suggested. "We could make them sprout arms and legs."

"Eyes could pop out!" Caleb exclaimed.

"And they could wear superhero capes," Zoe added. "Let's see how it hard it would be to make clay toothbrushes." She leaned back in her chair, balancing it on two legs. "Sonja, do you have extra modeling clay we could use?"

Sonja put down the clay were-snake she'd been working on and handed Zoe a couple blocks of the moldable clay.

"Thanks," Zoe said, letting the chair fall back in place.

"Sure," Sonja answered. The same grin she'd worn earlier broke across her face. "Hey, do you think the Ponies are all camped out in their bathrooms?" she asked, lowering her voice. "Do you think they'll be throwing up all night?"

Zoe frowned. She didn't like the Ponies either, but that didn't mean she wanted them all to be sick. Sonja sounded way too happy about the possibility.

"Principal Romero's note said ten people got sick. There are only five girls in the Ponies," Caleb said as he began shaping a toothbrush out of the clay.

"Emily got sick too," Sonja told him. "I'm not sure who else."

"Don't forget Leo," Jaden added, getting to work on a clay arm for their toothbrush movie star. "We saw him get sick. And Owen."

If they wanted it to look like the toothbrush was sprouting arms and legs, they'd need to make arms and legs in a bunch of different sizes. They'd have to take a picture of the toothbrush with really small arms and legs, then with arms and legs that gradually got bigger and bigger. That way, when the photos were turned into a movie, it would look like the toothbrush was actually growing the limbs.

"Bryce and Vic weren't in math," Goo volunteered from her place at Sonja's table. Goo's real name was Maya, but everyone called her Goo because she could answer most questions as fast as Google. She had one of those brains that let her remember everything she'd ever read, and Goo read *a lot*. "I heard they got sick in the hall when they were walking to class after lunch."

"That's ten," Sonja said. Her eyes widened. "It's everyone in the Ponies and everyone in the Inferior Five."

"But that would be eleven," Zoe reminded her. She looked up from working on clay eyeballs of different sizes that would make it look like eyes were popping out of the toothbrush. "Five Ponies, five Inferiors, plus Emily."

"Gabriel isn't in the Inferiors anymore," Sonja said, shaking her head. "He told me at lunch when he was handing out those fliers."

"Why?" Caleb asked. "He and Owen started up that group together, right?"

Goo shrugged. "He told me he was sick of comics," she answered. "He's getting rid of all of them, plus his action figures and other collectibles. I might buy some of the *Avengers vs. X-Men* series."

"Does he have #0?" Mrs. Ram asked as she walked over from the Things' table. "I missed that one, and I want to get my Hope Summers collection complete. She's my favorite mutant."

Zoe, Jaden, and Caleb exchanged grins. Mrs. Ram was so cool. She knew as much about comics as her students did — maybe even more. And she knew everything about science.

"Here's the list," Goo said, handing Mrs. Ram one of Gabriel's fliers. The teacher looked it over as she moved on and then sat down at another table to answer that group's questions.

"So since Gabriel isn't an Inferior anymore, all of the Ponies *and* all of the Inferiors got sick," Jaden said. "Plus Emily, who almost counts as one of the Ponies."

"It's so weird how fast it happened. We saw five of them get sick at almost exactly the same time," Zoe said. "Goo, what kind of sicknesses can pass between people really quickly?"

"The flu can pass from an infected person to someone as close as six feet away," Goo answered. "A lot of flu epidemics start in schools, because big groups of kids are close together."

"It doesn't seem like five people would get the flu in the same minute, though," Jaden commented. His brow furrowed the way it did when he was thinking hard.

Caleb jumped to his feet, dropping the clay toothbrush on the ground. "Poison!" he exclaimed. "Why didn't I think of it before? It's the only thing that makes sense. All the kids who got sick were poisoned!"

"It's not the *only* thing that makes sense," Zoe said firmly. She grabbed Caleb by the arm, pulled him back into his seat, picked up the toothbrush, and handed it to him. She wished he didn't always jump to the worst possible conclusion. "I guess it's one possible explanation, though."

"Goo, are there any poisons that would make you throw up right away?" Caleb asked.

"Some pesticides," Goo answered. "Ingredients in some cleaning products. And some mushrooms. That's all I know. I haven't read that much about poisons."

"See? Poisoning makes sense," Caleb told Zoe and Jaden.

"But what motive would someone have for poisoning the Ponies and the Inferiors?" Jaden asked, using a putty knife to carve fingers into the clay hand he was working on. He was a Sherlock Holmes fanatic and knew that motive, why a person would commit a crime, was key to solving any case. "There's no connection between those two groups, is there?"

"Not really," Zoe answered. "Owen is an Inferior, and his sister Olivia is a Pony. That's the only connection

I can think of. But I can't think of a reason someone would want to hurt *both* of them. They never hang out with the same people. They hardly even talk to each other at school."

Jaden frowned. "It seems more likely that we're looking for someone who has something against *all* the Inferiors and *all* the Ponies. After all, everyone in those groups was poisoned, not just Olivia and Owen. But I'm still stumped on a motive that makes sense."

"Me too," Caleb admitted. "But somebody out there wanted to hurt both those groups — and did!"

4

Wednesday morning, Zoe rushed into the media center and headed for the table where Jaden and Caleb were already sitting. They'd all decided to meet up that morning to work on their movie project since they hadn't gotten nearly enough done at their S.M.A.R.T.S. meeting the day before. They'd spent too much time talking about the possible poisoning.

They were all supposed to have made sketches of possible adventures for their toothbrush superheroes, but as Zoe flopped down, she said, "I'm so sorry. I know we said we'd all make sketches last night, but I didn't."

"I didn't do it either," Caleb admitted.

Jaden laughed. "We're the perfect team. I didn't do mine either. I couldn't stop trying to figure out how the Ponies and the Inferiors all got sick at the same time."

"Me too!" Zoe exclaimed.

"We know how — poison," Caleb said. "I spent all night trying to figure out who the poisoner could be, but I still couldn't think of anyone who'd have something against the Ponies *and* the Inferiors."

"The Inferiors pretty much stick together," Jaden said. "They don't even talk to that many other people."

"But not in a snobby way," Zoe added. "They're not mean to anyone — unlike the Ponies."

Jaden raised his eyebrows. "Good point. The Ponies treat a lot of people pretty terribly."

"Yeah, but if everybody the Ponies are mean to is a suspect, I'd be one," Zoe said. "Sonja would too. Yesterday . . ." She hesitated for a moment, not sure if she should continue. "Yesterday, when Sonja and I were walking to English, she said Isabella deserved to get sick and have a million bad things to happen to her. Emily and the rest of the Ponies too. And when we were talking about it yesterday in S.M.A.R.T.S., Sonja was smiling, like she was hearing great news."

"Can you think of any reason Sonja would want to hurt the Inferiors?" Jaden asked.

Zoe shook her head.

"So we have at least one suspect who could have wanted to poison the Ponies — Sonja — and no suspects who would want to hurt the Inferiors," Jaden said.

"Maybe we're thinking about the wrong kind of poisoning," Zoe suggested. "Maybe it was food poisoning, and no one was *trying* to make the Ponies or the Inferiors sick. It could have been an accident."

"But then more people would have gotten sick, right?" Caleb asked. "Lots of other people ate the cafeteria food. Most of the kids in second lunch didn't get sick, and no one in first lunch did."

"That's it!" Zoe exclaimed. "We need to find out what everyone who got sick ate and drank at lunch. Maybe there's something only the Inferiors and the Ponies had."

"Whatever made them sick, it doesn't seem too bad," Jaden said, nodding toward the windows along the left side of the media center. "Look, Olivia is already back at school."

Caleb glanced over. Jaden was right. Olivia was heading straight toward the media center. Instead of coming inside, though, she dropped a book into the book-drop and walked away, ponytail bobbing.

"That gives us a little new info," Jaden said. "The effects of the poison lasted less than twenty-four hours."

"Until I know exactly what happened, I don't even want to buy my apple juice in the cafeteria." Caleb pushed his fingers through his hair. "I'm not sure I even want to get water from the drinking fountain."

"What do you say, Sherlock?" Zoe asked Jaden. "Are the three of us taking the case? Everyone in school will feel better if we figure out why those kids got sick. And it might save Caleb's life. Dehydration is very serious."

Caleb swallowed hard. "How long can a person live without fluids?" he asked nervously.

Jaden rolled his eyes. Caleb was always convinced DOOM was around the corner. "You drank the apple juice yesterday and didn't get sick," he pointed out. "That means it wasn't poisonous. It's okay to drink —"

"This is horrible!" someone yelled from the front of the media center. "Mr. Leavey! Come quick! I found a note about what happened in the cafeteria yesterday!"

Mr. Leavey, the school librarian, popped out from between two rows of bookshelves and rushed toward the front counter. Zoe and Caleb rushed after him, Jaden following a little more slowly with the help of his braces.

"Calm down, Iris," Mr. Leavey told the teenage girl behind the media center checkout counter. "Take a deep breath." He smoothed down his tie, managing to get it stuck between two of the buttons on his shirt. Mr. Leavey kept the media center in perfect order but usually couldn't manage to keep himself equally neat.

Iris pulled in a long breath and let it out so slowly that Zoe started giving little hops of impatience. "I was checking in the books the way you showed me." Iris pulled in another breath. The teenage guy working behind the counter with her gave her a pat on the back.

"Iris and Harry are from the high school," Mr. Leavey explained to Jaden, Zoe, and Caleb as they waited for Iris to start talking again. "They're helping out here every morning this week as part of a work-experience program. There are groups of students volunteering in different parts of the school — the cafeteria, the office, the computer lab, the library. It gives them the chance to see what the jobs are like."

Iris let out another long, slow breath, then said, "I was checking in books — actually just one book. I'd already done all the ones in the book drop, but this one just got put in. And this fell out." She held up a folded slip of paper and began to take another long breath.

"You're okay, Iris," Harry said. "Are you sure the note was even about people getting sick?"

Mr. Leavey gently pulled the piece of paper from Iris's fingers. Caleb, Jaden, and Zoe were standing close enough to see what was written on it:

Yesterday you finally got some of what you deserve — all of you! That made me happy. Except responsibility and do what's right or something worse is going to happen.

Jaden felt sort of like he needed a deep breath himself. Who would write something like that? And what did that threat mean?

"Isn't it horrible?" Iris asked.

"It is," Mr. Leavey answered. He set the paper down on the counter. "You're looking a little pale, Iris. I'm going to go get you some water. Then I'm taking that note to the principal."

"That could be important evidence," Caleb whispered to Zoe and Jaden. He took out his cell and snapped a quick picture of the note.

Zoe turned to the high school kids. "Do you need help checking books in?" she offered. "Mr. Leavey lets me help sometimes. I could do these." She reached for the pile of books, each one about dog training, sitting on the counter.

"Those are mine," Harry said, stopping her. "Mr. Leavey's letting me borrow them. But thanks anyway."

There was nothing else they could do, so Zoe, Jaden, and Caleb returned to their table. "Olivia put a book in the drop slot about a minute before Iris started shouting," Jaden said as they sat down. "And Iris said there was only one book in the drop box. So the note had to be meant for Olivia, right? Do you think she saw it?"

Caleb looked at the picture he'd taken. "The note said, 'Yesterday you finally got what you deserve — all of you.' It sure sounds like the note was talking about Olivia and the rest of the Ponies; they're the only girls who got sick yesterday."

"Olivia is in my homeroom. I guess I could talk to her and see if she has any idea who sent the note — or if she even saw it," Zoe offered. Her stomach clenched a little at the thought. "I usually try to avoid all the Ponies, but this is our only real clue so far."

"Good idea," Jaden answered. "Caleb and I will print out the note. We'll need to examine it for clues."

"We have to be prepared for DOOM," Caleb told them. "The note made it sound like more bad stuff is going to happen. Something even worse than poisoning."

Jaden shook his head firmly. "Not if we can stop it."

5

It was still too early for Olivia to be going to homeroom, but Zoe knew the best way to find any of the Ponies was to find Isabella. With that in mind, she headed down the hallway toward Isabella's locker. Sure enough, Olivia stood at the end of the hall with Isabella and Nicole, another one of the Ponies.

They're just girls, Zoe told herself as she approached. *Just ordinary girls*. But her steps got slower and slower as she drew closer.

"Olivia, hi!" Zoe said when she was so close she had to say something. "There's something I need to tell you."

Despite the fact that the girls had gone to the same elementary school before starting at Hubble — and had even been in the same Brownie troop — Olivia shot Zoe a do-I-know-you look.

"Um, I was in the media center when you turned in your book," Zoe said. "The library aide found a note in it. It basically said that you and the other Ponies deserved to get sick yesterday. It also kind of said that more bad things were going to happen to all of you if you didn't start doing the right thing."

That got Isabella's attention. She held out her hand, palm up, as if waiting for Zoe to hand over the note.

"I don't have it," Zoe told her. "Mr. Leavey is taking it to the principal. But I thought Olivia should know what it said. All of you, actually, since part of it was a threat."

"I didn't even know it was there!" Olivia exclaimed. "Who would write something like that? That's awful!"

"I know. I couldn't believe it when I saw the note," Zoe said. She figured a little white lie was okay. After all, she needed to gather as much information as she could.

"I bet I know who sent it," Olivia burst out.

"Who?" Zoe asked.

Isabella shot her an annoyed look, and Zoe realized she needed to keep quiet and listen if she didn't want one of the girls telling her to leave.

"I bet it was that comic book geek," Isabella said.

"Gabriel," Olivia agreed. "That's exactly who I was thinking of."

"That makes total sense," Nicole agreed, flipping her ponytail. "Last week he asked us all to the fall dance, one after the other."

"Even Emily," Olivia agreed.

"When we all said no, he must have decided to get revenge!" Isabella exclaimed. "What was with him anyway? Why would he ever think one of us might say yes? Even Emily wouldn't go with him!"

Zoe shook her head, disgusted. The way they all kept saying "even Emily" was so mean. Like they thought she wasn't nearly up to the Ponies' standards.

"Speaking of Emily, where is she?" Nicole asked. "We're barely going to have time to drink our hot chocolates by the time she gets here."

"It's like remembering which one should have cinnamon and which one should have nutmeg is too much for her," Isabella said, rolling her eyes.

"Is Gabriel the only person you think might have sent the note?" Zoe interrupted.

Isabella gave her a long, cold look. "Are you saying other kids think we deserved to get sick yesterday?"

"No," Zoe said quickly, hoping it sounded convincing.

"Why are you still standing here, anyway?" Isabella said. "You told Olivia what you needed to tell her."

Zoe couldn't think of anything else to ask the girls, so she turned and walked away. She'd made it about halfway down the hall when Emily rushed past her holding a cardboard tray with what Zoe assumed were the Ponies' hot chocolates.

If Emily wanted to poison the Ponies, it would be easy for her. The snobby girls always expected her to fetch treats for them. But Emily wanted to be one of the Ponies, not hurt them — unlike Gabriel and Sonja. Now they had two suspects for poisoning the Ponies — but still none who might have wanted to poison the Inferiors.

The S.M.A.R.T.S. would figure it out, though. Zoe was sure of that. But there was part of her that wondered why they should even bother trying to discover who'd poisoned the Ponies. Why should they do anything nice for them when they were always so rotten to everyone else?

Zoe sighed. She knew the answer. Because it was the right thing to do.

6

"It's like Gabriel's had a brain transplant," Caleb said at lunch that day after Zoe had filled them in on her conversation with the Ponies. "First we find out he's selling his comics, then he starts dressing crazy, and now he's actually asking one of the Ponies to go to a dance."

"Not one, *all* of them," Zoe corrected.

"Did Olivia have any other ideas about who could have put the note in her book?" Jaden asked. "Anyone besides Gabriel?"

Zoe shook her head. "They were all offended I even asked. They clearly think everyone loves them as much as they love themselves."

Caleb gave a snort of laughter.

"Maybe we should follow through on Zoe's idea to figure out what all the kids who got sick ate," Jaden said. "Zoe, do you still have the video from yesterday's lunch on your phone? That's probably the best place for us to start."

Zoe nodded and got out her phone. Jaden and Caleb both leaned in closer, and she pressed play. They all peered at the tiny screen, trying to see what foods had been on the Ponies' and Inferiors' trays.

"I'm going to make a chart," Jaden said. "That way we can keep track of who ate what."

"Put us on too," Caleb suggested. "If we're talking food poisoning, we can eliminate everything the three of us ate or drank. None of us got sick."

"Good idea," Jaden said, pulling out a piece of paper and getting to work.

	Isabella	Nicole	Olivia	Jaycee	Amanda	Emry	Owen	Ryan	Mike	Leo	Jaden	Zoe	Caleb
EGG SALAD								X	X			X	
CHICKEN	X	X	X	X	X	X			X	X			
RICE	X	X	X	X	X	X	X	X			X		
BABY CARROTS				X	X					X	X		
SALAD	X	X			X	X			X			X	
MASH POTATO							X	X		X		X	
GRAVY							X			X	X		
PEACHES					X	X							
MIXED FRUIT	X	X	X	X			X			X	X		
MILK	X	X	X							X		X	X
APPLE JUICE				X	X	X	X	X		X	X		X

55

"All the Ponies ate almost exactly the same thing Isabella did," Jaden observed when they'd finished the chart.

"Of course they did," Zoe said, rolling her eyes. "They all *always* copy her. But look at the chart. Between the three of us, we ate all the foods the kids who got sick did."

Caleb ran his finger up and down the chart. "And there's not one food that everyone who got sick ate. That eliminates food poisoning, right?"

Jaden sighed. "Right. I read up on food poisoning last night — when I should have been working on my toothbrush sketches. Take chicken, for example. It can carry salmonella bacteria. If the cafeteria chicken was infected, every person who ate it might not get sick. But there's no reason someone who didn't eat it would have gotten sick — and there are plenty of people on our list who didn't eat chicken."

"Principal Romero must have already figured all that out," Zoe said, taking a bite of her bean-and-cheese burrito. "That's why she's keeping the cafeteria open and why she wrote the letter to parents saying the lunch food didn't make people sick."

"So we're back to someone intentionally poisoning both groups," Jaden said.

"Now we just have to figure out *who*," Caleb agreed, anxiously rolling his straw back and forth between his fingers. He hadn't even opened his apple juice.

"Let's switch it up and try thinking about *how* the poison was put into the food," Jaden said. "It might help if we focus on who had the opportunity to poison the food instead of who had a good motive."

"Maybe next we should map out the cafeteria," Caleb suggested. "If we know where everyone was, we'll know if they were close enough to poison the food."

Zoe nodded. "Good idea," she agreed. She hit play, and they re-watched the video of the cafeteria over and over until they had everyone's locations down.

"Why was Sonja behind the counter?" Caleb asked when the map was complete.

"I actually asked her that," Jaden told him. "She said she was back there to see if we could get popcorn for the viewing party next week when our movies are finished."

"I remember that," Zoe said, frowning. She didn't want Sonja to turn out to be the culprit. But still . . . "It wouldn't have been too hard for Sonja to slip something onto the plates. If she put poison on the plates, it wouldn't matter what food the Ponies and the Inferiors chose."

"We don't have a motive for her wanting to poison the Inferiors, though," Jaden pointed out.

"Not yet," Caleb answered. "But maybe she thought she'd look guilty if only the Ponies got sick. I mean, plenty of people have heard her say she doesn't like them. Maybe she thought no one would suspect her if she poisoned the Inferiors too."

"That's pretty cold," Zoe said.

"Well, poisoners aren't exactly nice people," Caleb told her.

"Sonja wasn't the only one standing behind the counter," Zoe reminded the guys. "We should find out more about the two cafeteria ladies. And isn't there a dishwasher, too?"

Jaden nodded. "I think we're on to something. It makes sense that the poison was added before everyone sat down. After all, the Ponies always sit by the windows, and the Inferiors always sit at the corner table in the back. Their tables are about as far apart as they can be. Once everyone was at their table, it would be hard to add poison to all their plates before they started eating."

"Everyone knows that the Ponies and Inferiors are always the first kids through the line," Zoe said. "So Sonja — or whoever the poisoner was — would know the Ponies and Inferiors would get the top plates on the stack. It'd be easy to just mess with those."

"We've got to figure out what really happened and fast," Caleb said, sounding worried. "We can't forget what the note said — something worse might be about to happen."

7

"Let's split up," Zoe said when she'd finished her last bite of lunch. "You two talk to the Inferiors about who might want to harm them, and I'll check out the situation back in the kitchen. Then we can all talk to Sonja after school. She'll probably be in the makerspace."

"Good idea," Jaden said. He looked over at Caleb, who was still staring at his unopened apple juice. "Are you going to drink that or what?"

"It's safe," Zoe told him. "You had it yesterday. I had it today." She shook her empty carton. "And I feel fine."

"I'm just not thirsty right now," Caleb said.

Zoe and Jaden looked at each other and shook their heads. Caleb always thought something awful was going to happen — usually DOOM. He didn't like to do anything that seemed even a little risky.

Jaden decided it was time for one of his jokes. Caleb could clearly use a laugh. "Hey, how do you make an apple turnover?" he asked.

"How?" Zoe asked.

"Push it down a hill," Jaden answered.

"Ha. Ha. Ha," Zoe said, rolling her eyes. But Caleb laughed, and that had been the whole point.

"Okay, then, let's go talk to the comics guys," Jaden said. The two boys got to their feet, and off they went.

Zoe stood up. As she crossed the cafeteria, she tried to think up an excuse that would allow her to get into the kitchen. By the time she got there, she had a plan.

"Hi, Ms. Padgett," Zoe said to the cafeteria lady behind the counter. "I'm in the S.M.A.R.T.S. club, and we're all making movies." She didn't mention that the movie would be stop-motion animation. "I wanted to practice filming things. Would it be okay if I took some video of the kitchen? We might have one in our movie."

Ms. Padgett pushed her curly red hair away from her face. "I suppose. We're finished serving. Come on around."

As Zoe made her way around the counter, a teenage boy with a cell phone pressed to his ear pushed through the swinging doors, almost plowing right into her.

"Felix, put your phone away, and watch where you're going," Ms. Padgett scolded.

"Gotta go. I'll leave in a minute," the boy mumbled, hanging up and putting his phone away. "Sorry," he said to Ms. Padgett.

The lunch lady shook her head and glanced at her watch. "Go ahead and leave. Clearly your girlfriend isn't going to survive another minute without you."

Felix grinned. "Thanks, Ms. Padgett. See you tomorrow."

Zoe whipped out her phone and got him on film before he left, then turned toward Ms. Padgett. "How long has Felix worked here?"

Mrs. Hadel, the other cafeteria lady, crinkled her nose. "Work? Is that what he does?"

"Be nice," Ms. Padgett said. "He's just a kid." She turned to Zoe. "Felix is just here for the week. A few of the high school kids are working at the middle school a few hours a day to get job experience. He helps us clean up and prep for second lunch once first lunch is served."

Zoe nodded. It was just like Iris and Harry helping Mr. Leavey in the media center every morning. "You don't think he does a good job, Mrs. Hadel?" she asked.

While she chatted, Zoe held up her phone, taking a panoramic shot of the kitchen. She made sure to get both Mrs. Hadel and Ms. Padgett on camera, hoping for clues. It would have been easy for either of them to put poison on the Ponies' and Inferiors' plates. It would have been easy for Felix too, but it didn't make sense. As far as Zoe knew, none of the three had any reason to want to hurt the kids.

"He'd do a better job if he was single, like the kid who helps us get ready for first lunch," Mrs. Hadel answered, wiping down the counter next to the dishwasher. "Felix is only here for an hour, and his girlfriend calls him twice in that time span. Once to make sure he got here okay — like walking over from the high school is dangerous — and once to make sure he's leaving on time."

Zoe smiled. The high school and the middle school were connected by a walkway. They weren't very far apart at all.

"He's probably her first boyfriend," Ms. Padgett commented.

Mrs. Hadel rolled her eyes and laughed. "You would have thought the world had ended on Monday when he realized his phone had run out of juice and he couldn't get her calls," she added.

Zoe turned slowly, trying to capture everything in the kitchen. She spotted a sign on the dishwasher that read *DO NOT USE* and made sure to get a close-up. "What's wrong with the dishwasher?" she asked.

"The repairman sure doesn't know," Mrs. Hadel said.

"It broke down Friday afternoon," Ms. Padgett explained. "The repairman has been out, but he hasn't been able to fix it yet. He needed to order a part."

"So how are you washing the dishes?" Zoe asked.

"The old-fashioned way — in the sink," Mrs. Hadel answered. "I wash them with soap and water and rinse them. Then I put them on that conveyer belt. The air dryer we're using until the washer is fixed can take ten plates at once, so it hasn't slowed things down too badly."

"It's a good week to have the high school volunteers," Ms. Padgett added. "Once the plates are on the conveyer belt, the volunteer sprays them with antibacterial spray and then rinses them with water." She pointed to the belt, and Zoe took video. "Then they go into the dryer. When the plates come out, I stack them on the racks until it's time to use them."

Zoe got video of the tall metal racks too.

"We want to make sure the plates get as clean as possible since we're doing them by hand right now. That's why we're using the antibacterial spray," Mrs. Hadel added. She tossed the cloth she'd been using to wipe the counter toward a big laundry basket — and missed.

"She's no basketball player," Ms. Padgett told Zoe. She bent down to retrieve the cloth, and something fell out of her apron pocket, bouncing on the floor with a little *click*.

Zoe leaned down to pick the object up. It was a pin made out of a paperclip with a paper flower on top. She'd made one for her mother in the fourth grade with her picture in the center of the flower. She turned the pin over — and saw Emily's picture.

Ms. Padgett snatched the pin away, carefully returning it to her pocket.

"I made one of those for my mom," Zoe said, trying to figure out why Ms. Padgett would have a picture of Emily Wade.

"Just tell her. She already saw it," Mrs. Hadel said.

"Emily is my daughter," Ms. Padgett told Zoe. "She kept her dad's name after he and I got divorced. I went back to my maiden name."

"Emily likes it that way, because she's embarrassed to have a cafeteria lady as a mother," Mrs. Hadel said, sounding upset. She grabbed another cloth and started wiping down one of the racks.

"She wouldn't be if it weren't for those horrible girls she's friends with," Ms. Padgett said, shaking her head. "She's changed so much since she started hanging around them. They treat her so badly, but she just won't see it."

"You mean the Ponies?" Zoe exclaimed.

Ms. Padgett nodded.

"That's too polite a name for them, in my opinion," Mrs. Hadel muttered to herself. She said it so quietly Zoe was sure she wasn't supposed to hear.

Zoe frowned. Could Ms. Padgett have poisoned the Ponies because she didn't like the way they treated her daughter? But that would mean she'd poisoned Emily, too. Ms. Padgett didn't sound as if she liked the way Emily had been acting, but a mother wouldn't poison her own daughter — would she?

8

"What are we supposed to say?" Caleb asked Jaden as they walked over to the Inferiors' table in the back of the cafeteria. "'Hi. Can you give us a list of people who hate you enough to poison you?'"

"Something like that, I guess," Jaden answered.

All the Inferiors looked up as the two boys approached their table. "So you guys all survived, huh?" Jaden asked. "We didn't think you'd be back in school already."

"I didn't think so either," Owen admitted. "That was some serious nastiness."

"But you're still eating the cafeteria food today," Caleb observed, holding his unopened apple juice.

"The principal said it was okay in that note she sent out," Leo told him. "She even called my parents. She said she'd gotten the food tested, and it wasn't contaminated. Besides, it's not like everyone who ate in the cafeteria yesterday got sick."

"It seems like it was just you guys and the Ponies," Jaden agreed. "One of the girls got a note saying they deserved it." He turned to Owen. "Your sister, actually."

"Olivia didn't say anything about it!" Owen exclaimed, looking a little queasy.

"She just got it this morning," Caleb said. "Did any of you get one? Since you got sick too, it seemed like maybe someone was out to get all of you."

Jaden glanced at the faces of all the Inferiors. He noticed Owen and one of the other guys, Bryce, exchanging a worried look. "Is there someone you can think of who'd want to hurt you?" he pressed.

"Gabriel!" Leo exclaimed, turning pale. "He knows we were right to kick him out of the group, but he —"

"You kicked Gabriel out of the Inferiors?" Caleb interrupted. "I thought he quit. How could you kick him out? I thought he started the group."

"The two of us did," Owen answered. "I didn't want to kick him out, but —"

"He stole my Clayface action figure," Leo jumped in. "There was no way we could let him stay after that."

"The one with switchable heads *and* arms?" Caleb asked. "And the blue power crystals sprouting over his body?"

Leo nodded. "Yeah. I told Gabriel he could look at it during our last meeting.

He swears he put it back in my backpack before we left Owen's — that's where we have the meetings. But it wasn't there."

"We told Gabriel he had to empty out his backpack, and he refused to do it," Owen added. "He just got all mad because he said we should trust him, and then he stormed out. He had to have it with him. We searched every room in my house looking for it."

"We even got Ogre, Owen's dog, to help us," Bryce said. "The McGuires have to keep everything out of his reach because he likes to grab stuff. If the Clayface had been

buried in the couch or dropped somewhere, Ogre would have sniffed it out."

"I really hate that guy. I —" Leo didn't finish. He couldn't. He'd started puking.

A second later, Owen bolted up out of his seat and raced toward the bathroom.

Across the room, Isabella ran out of the cafeteria too, a napkin pressed over her mouth.

Within a few minutes, ten kids had gotten sick. The same ten kids as the day before.

They'd been poisoned — again!

9

"Now we have a suspect with motive for poisoning the Inferiors and the Ponies," Jaden said when he, Zoe, and Caleb had gathered in the makerspace Wednesday afternoon. "Gabriel — he got rejected by the Ponies *and* kicked out of the Inferiors."

"Sonja or Ms. Padgett also might have poisoned the Inferiors to make themselves look less guilty," Zoe said. She gave the boys a quick rundown of everything she'd seen in the kitchen. "Poisoning some other kids would make it look like the Ponies weren't really the target."

"So now what?" Caleb asked. He picked up a piece of clay and started making another toothbrush. So far, they were the only S.M.A.R.T.S. kids in the makerspace. Mrs. Ram sat a few tables away grading papers. She tried to be in there most days so kids could use the makerspace even when there weren't official S.M.A.R.T.S. meetings.

"We need evidence," Jaden answered.

"Did you guys notice anything in the note that gave you any clues?" Zoe asked. The discovery of the note felt so long ago. So much had happened since then. The same ten kids from the day before had gotten sick in the cafeteria again. Just those ten. No one else.

"The note said 'except responsibility,'" Jaden said. "E-x-c-e-p-t. That's the wrong word. It should have been a-c-c-e-p-t. That's the one that means to take responsibility."

"So whoever wrote the note didn't know the difference," Caleb added.

Jaden nodded. "We might have been able to get some info from the type of pen used if we had the original," he continued. "But not with a copy."

"My mom believes in graphology," Zoe said. "She thinks you can tell a person's personality by their handwriting. Like if someone writes with big letters, it means they're outgoing." She took the clay eyeballs she'd been working on out of a plastic storage container. "I keep trying to tell her that it's been proven graphology is a junk science, but she insists it works."

"But I've seen scientists on TV testify about whether a document is fake or not," Caleb said. "Everyone writes differently, and they examine stuff like how far apart the letters are and if they're more rounded or pointy."

"That's different than being able to tell somebody's personality from the way they write," Jaden said. He pulled the copy of the note out of his backpack and laid it out on the table so they could all see it.

"The letters mostly slant a little to the left," Zoe observed.

"And the writing switches back and forth between cursive and printing," Jaden pointed out. "The *p*'s and the *t*'s are printed, but the rest of the letters are cursive."

"We need to see Sonja's and Gabriel's handwriting," Caleb said. He squeezed the clay toothbrush too hard, accidentally breaking it in half.

"We need to see samples from all our suspects. That means Ms. Padgett too," Zoe said.

"Tomorrow we can probably look at Sonja's homework and —" Jaden started to say.

He was interrupted by Mr. Leavey, who rushed into the makerspace at that moment. Somehow one of his pant legs had gotten stuck in his sock.

"Mrs. McGuire just called!" the librarian exclaimed, heading toward Mrs. Ram's table.

"Are Olivia and Owen all right?" she asked.

"Yes, yes. The symptoms seem to be fading quickly, the way they did yesterday," Mr. Leavey answered. "The reason she called is that Owen found a threatening note in one of his library books. It said almost the same thing that note in Olivia's book did."

"Both notes in library books instead of their text books or backpacks or lockers," Jaden said.

Zoe looked from Jaden to Caleb. "Does that mean anything?"

"I'm not sure. But we shouldn't overlook it. In 'The Bascombe Valley Mystery,' Sherlock Holmes said his method was 'founded upon the observation of trifles,'" Jaden answered. "He'd say no detail was too small to be important."

"Okay, so the notes were in library books," Caleb said. "Maybe that means the notes were put into the books while the books were in the library."

"I've helped Mr. Leavey check out books before," Zoe said. "The computer shows what time each book

81

is checked out. The records might tell us some of the people who were in the library when Olivia and Owen checked out their books. At least it would tell us who else checked out books around the same time."

"Let's do it," Jaden said.

Zoe stood up and walked over to the table where Mr. Leavey and Mrs. Ram were sitting. "Mr. Leavey, Caleb and Jaden are interested in seeing how the media center computer works," she said. "Is it okay if I show them?"

"Yes, yes, fine," Mr. Leavey replied, sounding distracted. "Call me if anyone comes up to the desk."

"I will." Zoe motioned to the boys, then led the way behind the checkout counter. She typed "McGuire, Olivia" into the space for the borrower's name and watched as the computer worked its magic.

"The last book she checked out was on Monday morning," Zoe said. "But we don't know if that's the book the note was in."

"Look to see when Owen checked out a —" Caleb began.

But just then, Jaden's eyes fell on a piece of paper sitting on the counter. The handwriting on it looked familiar. He picked it up to get a better look. "Don't bother," he said. "I know who wrote the note."

"What?" Zoe burst out.

"Who?" Caleb demanded.

"Harry, the high school guy working in the library this week," Jaden said. "He left this note for Mr. Leavey." He held it up so the other two could see.

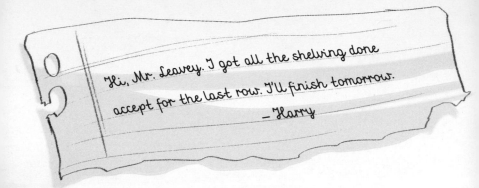

Hi, Mr. Leavey. I got all the shelving done accept for the last row. I'll finish tomorrow.
— Harry

"The *p*'s and *t*'s are printed and the rest is cursive." Caleb turned to Jaden. "You're a genius, dude."

"He got *except* and *accept* wrong again too," Zoe said. "But the other way around."

"We have our poisoner!" Caleb exclaimed, pumping his fist in the air. "Case closed."

Zoe started to give a fist pump of her own, then stopped. "Wait. Wait, wait, wait. Harry couldn't have been the poisoner."

"What?" Caleb exclaimed. "Why not?"

"Because he wasn't in the cafeteria," Zoe explained. "That means he wasn't anywhere near the food or plates!"

"You're right," Jaden said with a frustrated sigh. "But he wrote the note to Olivia and probably the one to Owen. I don't get why he'd do that."

Caleb stuck his fingers in his hair and gave it a tug. "This case is impossible!"

10

"I'm going down to the principal's office to tell her about the note Owen found," Mr. Leavey said as he passed Jaden, Zoe, and Caleb on their way back to their table. "If anyone needs help, Mrs. Ram is covering for me."

"Now what?" Caleb asked as they sat down. He didn't even bother to return to work on the toothbrush. He needed all his brainpower for the mystery.

Zoe and Jaden seemed to feel the same way. "Well, there's no reason to look for handwriting samples from any of our other suspects. We know who wrote the note now," Jaden answered.

"And it's someone who can't be the poisoner," Zoe said. "I'm so confused!"

Caleb's eyes widened. "I just realized something — the note we saw didn't actually *talk* about the poisonings. It didn't even say anything about the Ponies or Inferiors."

"Yeah, it did. It said they all got what they deserved," Zoe said.

Jaden shook his head. "Caleb's right. It didn't say poisoning. When Iris found the note, we all figured it was about the poisoning, because it had happened the day before. But maybe the timing was just a coincidence. Maybe the note had nothing to do with the Ponies and Inferiors getting sick in the cafeteria."

"It's like the pictures Mrs. Ram showed us," Caleb said. "We assumed the dog wanted the steak or the ball because she showed us the pictures together."

"The sequence fooled us." Jaden shook his head. "Sherlock wouldn't have made an assumption like that."

"Olivia and Owen both got notes," Zoe said. "They're sister and brother. Do you think Harry could have something against the McGuires? The note said 'all of you.' That could mean a family instead of the Ponies and Inferiors."

"It's possible," Jaden said. "Maybe he —"

Caleb suddenly let out a groan that stopped Jaden mid-sentence. "Can we please focus on solving one mystery at a time? Before we figure out what's going on with Harry, let's figure out who poisoned the Ponies and Inferiors."

Just then, Sonja walked into the makerspace. "Hey, guys," she said, sitting down at her usual table. "Can you believe people got sick in the caf again? I'm not eating food from there ever again. Today I brought my lunch and ate in the bathroom."

"I don't blame you," Caleb said.

"I know it's scary, people getting sick two days in a row," Mrs. Ram said, overhearing them. "But Principal Romero is working really hard to figure out what happened. I promise she's going to make sure the cafeteria is safe."

"No one got sick during first lunch this time either, right?" Sonja asked Mrs. Ram.

Mrs. Ram nodded. "Second lunch only, and only a small percentage of the students," she answered before returning to grading papers.

"Let me ask again: what do we do now?" Caleb said.

Zoe lowered her voice to a whisper. "We still have our suspects." She gave a tiny nod in Sonja's direction. "But we don't have any proof that one of them did it."

"How about if we use the storyboard software to map out everything we know?" Jaden suggested. "Maybe we'll realize there's a detail we missed."

They hadn't used the software yet, but Mrs. Ram had given them a brief tutorial on it the day they'd started the movie project. She'd wanted all the groups to plan out their movies using storyboards — drawings of each shot in a movie — to make sure everything in the movie was in order before filming started.

Caleb got up. "Good idea. I'll grab one of the laptops."

"Okay, first thing we know about the past two days is that the Inferiors — minus Gabriel — and the Ponies were first in line."

"That's what happens every day," Zoe commented.

"Today it was the Inferiors," Jaden continued. "Yesterday it was the Ponies." He began making a sketch with those ten kids at the front of the line.

Zoe shook her head. "Wait, that's not the first thing we know. Before anyone got to the cafeteria for second lunch, Ms. Padgett, Mrs. Hadel, and Felix were working in the kitchen. Mrs. Hadel said Felix always gets a phone call when he first arrives." She drew a sketch of Felix on the phone looking goofy with hearts floating over his head.

"The three of them were washing dishes from first lunch. Mrs. Hadel washed and rinsed the plates in the sink, then put them on a conveyer belt. She said she did them ten at a time, because that's what the air dryer held." Zoe sketched some more. "Felix sprayed them with antibacterial solution and rinsed them. Then they went into the dryer. After that, Ms. Padgett moved them to the racks until it was time to use them."

Caleb came back with the computer and camera and started photographing and uploading the sketches. "Put the one with Felix on the phone first. That's the beginning of the sequence," Zoe told him.

"Okay, so then the Inferiors and the Ponies move down the food line. Ms. Padgett and Mrs. Hadel put the food on the plates," Jaden said as he drew.

"They always wear rubber gloves," Caleb said as he started clicking and dragging the photos he'd uploaded. The software made it easy to change the order. "That's something I look for. I don't want anyone's hands except mine touching my food."

"The Ponies go over to their table. The Inferiors go over to theirs," Jaden continued. He drew a sketch of the Inferiors walking toward the back of the cafeteria while Zoe drew one of the Ponies walking toward a table by the windows. Caleb photographed and uploaded the drawings.

"What else?" Jaden asked.

"We forgot to put Sonja in one of the sketches," Zoe whispered. Sonja seemed completely wrapped up in working on her movie, but Zoe didn't want her to overhear.

Caleb slapped his hands on the table. "She wasn't back there both days! We didn't even think of that!"

"Quiet," Zoe reminded him.

Caleb lowered his voice. "Sonja wasn't near the food yesterday. On Tuesday she was because she was asking about the popcorn, but not today."

"You're right — she said she brought her lunch and ate in the bathroom," Zoe said softly. Relief swept through her. She really hadn't wanted to believe Sonja would hurt anyone on purpose.

"On the map we made, Gabriel was sitting by himself at a table near the door," Jaden said. "That's about as far away from the Ponies and the Inferiors as possible."

He studied the storyboards Caleb had created on the computer. "Anything else?"

"Can't think of anything," Zoe said.

"Okay, let's see what we can figure out from the sketches," Jaden suggested.

All three of them stared at the storyboards in silence for several long moments.

"I got nothing," Caleb finally said.

"Me either," Jaden admitted.

Zoe sighed. "Me either either. Maybe we should email ourselves the storyboards. We can all look at them again tonight."

"Good idea. Let's meet here before school tomorrow," Jaden suggested. "That way we can talk to Harry and keep trying to figure out *how* people are getting poisoned and *who's* doing the poisoning."

11

"Keep our kids safe! Keep our kids safe! Keep our kids safe!"

Caleb heard the chants as soon as he got off the bus Thursday morning. His heart lurched in his chest as he caught sight of the crowd of parents that had gathered on the lawn. They all held signs with phrases like: *Hubble Flunks Health!* and *Cafeteria Food = Vomit!* and *Save Our Kids!* written on them.

A woman with a big camera on her shoulder was getting the whole thing on film, while a reporter Caleb recognized from the local news was yelling questions.

Principal Romero strode out the main doors, and all the parents booed.

DOOM! Total DOOM! Caleb ran to the media center and burst inside, heading straight for the makerspace. He found Jaden and Zoe sitting there quietly. The rest of the tables were empty.

"Did you see what's going on outside?" Caleb yelled.

"Yeah," Jaden answered.

"Kind of hard to miss," Zoe added.

"Well, what are we going to do?" Caleb demanded.

"That's why we're meeting. To figure it out," Jaden reminded him.

"Let's go talk to Harry. Mr. Leavey said he'd be working at the library every morning this week," Zoe said. "At least that's one mystery we've solved. Well, sort of. We know he wrote those mean notes, we just don't know why."

"On it!" Caleb took off for the checkout desk.

"He's entered The Zone," Jaden said. That's what he and Zoe called it when Caleb got so worked up about something that he could hardly function. He definitely couldn't stand still and have a conversation.

"We know you wrote notes to Olivia and Owen!" Jaden and Zoe heard Caleb yell as they started after him. "Why did you threaten them? Why would you be glad they got hurt? What's wrong with you?"

"I — what? I don't even know what you're talking about," Harry answered.

By the time Zoe and Jaden caught up with him, Caleb looked like he was ready to climb over the check-in counter to get to Harry. Zoe grabbed the hood of Caleb's sweatshirt and pulled him back a few steps.

"We compared the handwriting on your note to Mr. Leavey to the writing on the note to Olivia," Jaden told Harry calmly. "The slant and the size of the letters match, plus you misused the words *accept* and *except* in both of them."

Harry started to blink really quickly. Iris, the high school girl working with him at the desk, started doing deep breathing.

"And you print some letters and write some in cursive," Zoe chimed in. "The same letters in both notes." She slowly released Caleb's hoodie.

"I — I — it's their fault!" Harry cried. "The McGuires' stupid dog keeps crawling under the fence and digging huge holes in my backyard. He's buried stuff everywhere out there! Every time I practice soccer out there I fall in one of them. I even had to miss an important match, because I twisted my ankle stepping into one of those stupid holes!"

"You said in the letter that they deserved the pain they got. What did you do?" Caleb asked. He didn't care about Harry's excuses.

"My dad called the police. They came by and gave the McGuires a warning. Olivia was really upset. I saw her start crying because she thought they would take Ogre — that's the dog's name — away," Harry explained. "Owen kept hugging Ogre like he was scared he was going to lose him. But did they fix the fence? No. There was more stuff buried in our yard the next day. I have a whole pile of stuff from out there — a cat toy, three different shoes, my baseball glove, an Abominable Snowman doll, my brother's chemistry book."

Harry was working himself into The Zone, talking faster and faster and louder and louder. "I'm going to get kicked off the team if I can't practice at home!" he practically yelled. "I read some books about training dogs, but Ogre is too dumb to bother trying. I was just trying to get the McGuires to keep the dog where he belongs."

"What's going on out here?" Mr. Leavey asked, walking out of his office. "I was on the phone with a parent. Why all the yelling?"

Jaden quickly explained about Harry being the one who had written the threatening notes.

"Is this true, Harry?" Mr. Leavey asked. Iris sat down and kept taking deep breaths.

"Yes. But that dog —" Harry started to say.

Mr. Leavey held up his hand to stop him. "I'm going to have to talk to our principal about this," he told Harry. "You need to head back to the high school. Now, please." The librarian turned to Iris. "Can you handle things while I call the high school?"

Iris nodded. Mr. Leavey hurried off to call the high school principal.

Harry grabbed his jacket and came out from behind the counter. "It really is the McGuires' fault," he muttered as he headed for the door.

"Wait! Abominable Snowman doll!" Zoe suddenly exclaimed. She jumped in front of Harry, blocking his way, and whipped out her phone, quickly pulling up a picture of the Clayface action figure. "Did it look like this?"

Clayface might look sort of like a hairless Abominable Snowman to someone who wasn't into comics. The crystals he sprouted that gave him extra powers kind of looked like blue ice.

Harry glanced at the phone. "Yeah. That's it." With that, he circled around her and left.

Zoe walked over to Jaden and Caleb and showed them her cell. "Gabriel didn't steal it!" she said. "Ogre did! Didn't you say that the Inferiors told you they meet at the McGuires' house?"

Jaden nodded. "They also said the McGuires have to keep stuff out of Ogre's reach so he won't grab things! The Inferiors kicked Gabriel out for nothing!" he exclaimed. Using his stronger hand, he exchanged fist bumps with Caleb and Zoe. "We figured out the mystery of who sent the notes — and why. Now we just have to figure out who the poisoner is."

"We could look at the storyboards again," Zoe suggested. "But I kept looking at them last night and didn't get any ideas."

"I kept looking at them too," Caleb said. "I got nothing."

"Same with me," Jaden answered.

"Maybe we missed a step in the sequence," Zoe suggested. "Our storyboards could have a gap, something none of us noticed."

"Maybe something that happened before we got there," Caleb said. "The cafeteria ladies told Zoe what was going on in the kitchen between when they finished serving first lunch and started serving second lunch, but maybe there's something they accidently left out."

Jaden looked from Zoe to Caleb. "Think you can figure out a way to get out of your third-period classes early?"

"I'm an excellent fibber. I'll come up with something," Zoe told them.

"I'll get to the cafeteria before first lunch ends somehow," Caleb said.

"We're going to figure this out," Jaden promised. "Before one kid takes another bite of poisoned food."

12

"Hi, Ms. Padgett! Hi, Mrs. Hadel!" Zoe called from the student side of the counter. "Would it be okay if I did a little more filming? I brought a couple helpers."

Mrs. Hadel frowned. "It's not a very good day."

"We won't get in the way," Jaden promised.

Mrs. Hadel sighed and shrugged. "Okay," she said. "But you have to leave before we start serving."

"Definitely," Caleb agreed. He, Jaden, and Zoe went into the kitchen and stood by the broken dishwasher so they'd be out of the way.

Zoe filmed Mrs. Hadel as she filled one side of the double sink with hot water and added dishwashing soap. She filled the other side of the sink with clean water for rinsing. Felix came in the door just as Mrs. Hadel started washing the first dish.

"That's the high school guy who is helping this week," Zoe whispered to Jaden and Caleb.

After Mrs. Hadel washed and rinsed a dish, she set it on a conveyer belt. The rubber belt had holes about the size of pennies in it, and a long metal trough ran underneath. Zoe figured the trough must be to hold the water after it ran off the plates — Felix would be rinsing them after he coated them with antibacterial spray.

Felix took his place alongside the conveyer belt. He held a large container of antibacterial spray in one hand. In the other hand, he held the nozzle of a hose that hung above the conveyer belt.

"Coming at you!" Mrs. Hadel called. She pressed a button, and the dishes slowly began moving toward Felix. Zoe did a quick count. Ten plates in the batch, just like the cafeteria ladies had said.

Felix began spraying the plates with the antibacterial solution. Just then his phone rang, and he answered it, continuing to spray.

"That's his girlfriend," Zoe told Caleb and Jaden. "She calls to make sure he gets over here okay."

"What is he, three years old?" Caleb muttered.

Felix kept disinfecting the plates. But when they continued down the conveyer belt, he didn't spray them with the hose. They moved down the belt into the air dryer. "I gotta go," he told his girlfriend. "See you in math." He hung up and stuck his phone in his pocket.

Ten new plates moved down the belt. Felix shot the antibacterial spray at them, then used the hose to spray them off. As the first ten plates came out of the air dryer, Ms. Padgett moved them to the top row of the tall metal dish rack.

"Stop!" Zoe cried. "You didn't rinse the first batch!"

Ms. Padgett, Mrs. Hadel, and Felix all froze.

"What's in that spray?" Jaden exclaimed. "Is it something that could make someone sick?"

"Oh, no! Oh, no!" Ms. Padgett cried. She rushed over to a clipboard hanging on the wall. "We have safety sheets for every product we use in the kitchen." She flipped through the pages. "Here it is — Germ-Away." She began to read aloud from the sheet. "Health effects: oral ingestion may result in gastrointestinal irritation with nausea, vomiting, and diarrhea."

"That sounds pretty much like the last two days in the caf," Caleb observed.

"I poisoned those kids? Did I poison those kids?" Felix's face had gone gray.

"It was an accident," Ms. Padgett said.

"You only forgot to rinse the plates when you were on the phone with your girlfriend," Zoe said. She felt bad for him. He hadn't meant to hurt anyone.

"And you always take the plates from the top of the rack when you start serving the food, right?" Caleb asked

Ms. Padgett. She nodded. "That's why the first ten kids in line got sick both days," he said.

"You're only on the phone when you first get here, when your girlfriend calls. And it's only for a short time, not even a minute. So it's only the first batch of dishes that didn't get the Germ-Away rinsed off," Jaden said.

"And on Monday you didn't get a call, because your cell phone was dead!" Zoe exclaimed, remembering what Mrs. Hadel had said. "That's why no one got sick then! You didn't get distracted."

Ms. Padgett quickly began taking the dishes off the tall rack. "We'll need to wash these again. And I'll need to go talk to Principal Romero. She'll be so relieved to know that we — I mean you three" — she said to Caleb, Zoe, and Jaden — "figured out why kids kept getting sick."

"I'm going to get expelled," Felix whispered.

"No, you won't," Ms. Padgett said firmly. "I'll explain that it was an accident. Principal Romero will understand."

* * *

Half an hour later, Jaden, Zoe, and Caleb were sitting in the cafeteria. Mrs. Hadel and Ms. Padgett had told them they could have whatever they wanted for lunch as a thank-you. Caleb had asked for a tuna sandwich and was happily eating it. "Might even be better than the ones I bring from home," he admitted.

Zoe took another bite of her spaghetti with extra meatballs. "Look at Gabriel," she said, nodding toward the Inferiors' table. "He's back where he belongs."

"I bet he'll have one of his thrift store T-shirts on tomorrow," Caleb said.

"May I join you?" Mrs. Ram asked, sitting down next to Jaden. "I had to tell you all how proud I am of you. I heard what happened from the principal. So tell me everything. How did you figure it out?"

"We studied the sequence of events," Zoe said.

"Kind of like we've been doing working on our movie. We even did storyboards!" Caleb added.

"If just one part of the sequence had been different, everything would have changed," Jaden explained. "If

Felix's girlfriend hadn't called him right when he got to work, he wouldn't have forgotten to rinse the plates."

"On Monday his phone was dead, so he didn't get distracted, and nobody got sick," Zoe added.

"If the Ponies and the Inferiors didn't always fight to be first in line, different kids might have gotten sick," Jaden said.

"And if the dishwasher hadn't broken down, antibacterial spray wouldn't have been used at all. If it had broken down a different week, high school kids wouldn't have been working at our school, and Felix wouldn't have been working with the plates. Without all those small events, no one would have gotten sick. Sequence, sequence, sequence," Zoe finished.

"One little change and ka-boom!" Caleb threw his arms out wide. "DOOM!"

"But also, a different little change, and everything's great," Zoe told him.

Mrs. Ram smiled at the three of them. "I'm just glad you three ended up in the sequence."

13

Zoe grabbed Jaden's arm with one hand and Caleb's with the other. Their movie was about to start! They'd decided not to use the toothbrush superhero idea after all, and they couldn't wait to see what the rest of the S.M.A.R.T.S. thought of the film they'd come up with.

A little more than a week had passed since they'd solved the cafeteria mystery, and the S.M.A.R.T.S. were showing the stop-motion movies they'd made — while eating popcorn. Mr. Leavey usually didn't allow food in the media center, but he'd agreed that the screening of everyone's movies was a special occasion.

On the screen, five ponies with bright ribbons in their manes and tails *clip-clopped* their way into the school cafeteria. Caleb, Zoe, and Jaden had thought about using audio file for the *clip-clopping* sound, but Jaden had found an article online about how when movies were first being made, the sound of horses hooves was created using coconut shells, so that's what they'd done. They'd recorded the sound of two empty coconut halves banging together, and it really did sound like horses.

They'd chosen to use *My Little Pony* action figures, each one a different color, for the horses. They'd had to take hundreds of photos to create the illusion that the ponies were walking to the front of the food line. They'd been super careful to move the ponies forward only a tiny bit between each picture. If they moved them too much between photos, the horses moved in a jerky way when the photos were turned into film.

The first pony, pink with flowing yellow hair, gave its food order. Zoe had recorded the dialogue herself, then experimented with voice-changing software until she found a voice that sounded horsey to her.

The cafeteria lady scooped a pile of hay onto a plate. Jaden, Zoe, and Caleb had used the film Zoe had taken with her cell phone as a reference while they'd worked to create a miniature version of the cafeteria. It had taken a lot of supplies: cardboard, popsicle sticks, pieces of clear

plastic from recycled water bottles, pieces of metal from recycled cans, modeling clay, pipe cleaners, and tons of other stuff they found in the makerspace. Zoe had even raided her old dollhouse for tiny plates and utensils.

The first pony picked up the plate of hay — they'd had to use a hot glue gun to keep the plate in place because it kept falling out of the pony's little mouth — and trotted away. The next pony moved up to give her order. Zoe had chosen a slightly different voice effect for it so each pony would sound unique.

"That speckled one has to be Nicole, because —" Thing One called out.

"— the speckles are like her freckles," Thing Two finished.

Caleb grinned. He'd been the one who'd used a marker to draw the speckles on one of the plastic ponies. He'd had to coat the plastic with acrylic floor wax first, otherwise the marker kept wiping off.

"But there should be six ponies," Goo said. "Or five and one half-pony, half-girl mutant."

"For Emily, you mean?" Sonja asked. Goo nodded.
"You have to look up from your books once in a while,
Goo. Emily hasn't been hanging around the Ponies
anymore. When they found out her mom was one of the
cafeteria ladies, they said some really mean things to
her. I guess that was the last straw, because she totally
ditched them. She might even join S.M.A.R.T.S."

"We'd make better friends," Zoe said.

"*Shhhh!*" Caleb shushed them.

When the Inferiors came onto the screen — all five
of them   there was more laughing and cheering. Jaden,
Zoe, and Caleb had made clay figurines of all the boys
based on illustrations from the comic books. At first the
clay arms and legs and heads kept coming off, but then
Jaden had come up with the idea to make wire frames to
use under the clay. That had worked great!

Jaden, Zoe, and Caleb were happy they'd decided
to ditch the superhero toothbrush idea and do a movie
based — sort of — on their own lives. They'd even done
one scene of themselves. They'd gotten Goo to take a

whole bunch of pictures of the three of them pointing to the label on a bottle of Germ-Away while making horrified faces.

It had been a lot harder to make the tiny changes in position themselves than it had been to move the plastic ponies and clay Inferiors around. Their movements had come out sort of choppy. But they'd agreed it still looked cool — like they were action figures themselves.

When the movie credits began to roll, the whole group, including Mrs. Ram and Mr. Leavey, applauded.

"That was great, you three," Mrs. Ram said. "But I didn't notice a title. What are you going to call it? Every great movie needs a great title."

Caleb, Jaden, and Zoe exchanged a look and announced: *"The Case of the Poison Plates!"*

About the Author

Melinda Metz is the author of more than sixty books for teens and kids, including *Echoes* and the young adult series Roswell High, the basis of the TV show *Roswell*. Her middle-grade mystery *Wright and Wong: Case of the Nana-Napper* (co-authored by the fabulous Laura J. Burns) was a juvenile Edgar finalist. Melinda lives in Concord, North Carolina, with her dog, Scully, a pen-eater just like the dog who came before her.

About the Illustrator

Heath McKenzie is a best-selling author and illustrator from Melbourne, Australia. Over the course of his career, he has illustrated numerous books, magazines, newspapers, and even live television. As a child, Heath was often inventing things, although his inventions didn't always work out as planned. His inventions still only work some of the time . . . but that's the fun of experimenting!

Glossary

agitated (AJ-uh-tay-ted) — made nervous and worried

contaminated (kuhn-TAM-uh-nay-ted) — made unfit to use because something dirty or harmful was added

disinfect (dis-in-FEKT) — to kill germs using chemicals

examine (eg-ZAM-in) — to look at something carefully

motive (MOH-tiv) — the reason why a person did something

offended (uh-FEND-ed) — made hurt or angry by someone's actions or words

revenge (ri-VENJ) — the act of getting back at someone for something they did to you or a person you care about

salmonella (sal-muh-NEL-uh) — a type of bacteria sometimes found in food that has not been cooked or handled properly. The bacteria can cause a person to become sick.

sequence (SEE-kwuhnss) — the order in which things happen

suspect (SUHS-pekt)— a person who is believed to have done something wrong

technique (tek-NEEK) — a way of doing something that takes skill and practice

threat (THRET) — a warning that something bad will happen if a certain thing is done or not done

Discussion Questions

1. Imagine you are a member of S.M.A.R.T.S. How would you have gone about solving the case of the poison plates? Talk about your plan and different options.

2. The Ponies and the Inferiors are just two of the groups at Hubble Middle School. Does your school have any similar groups? Talk about what they are and what makes them unique.

3. If just one element in the sequence of events had changed, everything in this book might have turned out differently. Talk about a time in your life when sequence was important.

Writing Prompts

1. Pretend you're in S.M.A.R.T.S. and have been assigned a stop-motion movie. Create a storyboard that shows how your movie would play out.

2. Even though Harry was angry with Owen and Olivia's family, writing those notes still wasn't a good idea. Put yourself in Harry's shoes, and write an apology note to both kids.

3. Many people believe that you can tell a lot about a person from their handwriting. In fact, Harry's handwriting is what ultimately gave him away. Do you think graphology is a real science? Write a paragraph explaining your opinion and your reasoning.

Stop-Motion

Stop-motion is a type of film technique where you make an object look like it's moving by taking photographs of it in slightly different positions. The photos are then shown in a rapid sequence to create the illusion of movement. This illusion is possible because humans have a limit to how much we can see and notice. When the photographs are shown quickly one after the other and the changes between each photo are very small, the eye and brain don't notice the individual pictures. Instead you see one continuous movement.

Sometimes whole films are made using stop-motion animation, such as *The Nightmare Before Christmas* or *Coraline*. Although you could use any object in stop-motion, clay figures are used the most because they're easy to work with and your characters can show more emotion. Movies that use clay figures and stop-motion are often called Claymation films. Not many movies are made with stop-motion, though, partly because it's a very slow and time-consuming process. It can take about a week to make one to two minutes of finished film.

Other times stop-motion is used for only parts of movies. In the original Star Wars trilogy, some aliens and machines were brought to life using stop-motion animation. Poseable models or puppets were photographed separately from the people and then, through various film techniques, were added later into the final movie. This was an especially popular special effect that directors used before computer graphics were available.

More adventure and science mysteries!

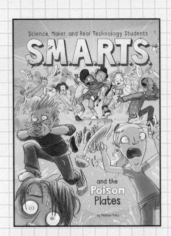

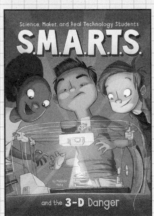

www.capstonepub.com